This magical book belongs to:

....

twinkly lights

balloons

party hats

birthday cake

birthday bunting

lanterns

fairy friends

surprise present

First published in 2016 by Hodder and Stoughton
This paperback edition published in 2017

Hodder Children's Books, an imprint of Hachette Children's Group, part of Hodder and Stoughton
Carmelite House, 50 Victoria Embankment, London, EC4Y 0DZ
Hodder Children's Books Australia, Level 17/207 Kent Street, Sydney, NSW 2000

The right of Katharine Holabird to be identified as the author and
Sarah Warburton as the illustrator of this Work has been asserted by them
in accordance with the Copyright, Designs and Patents Act 1988.

A catalogue record of this book is available from the British Library.

ISBN: 978 1 444 91967 7

An Hachette UK Company
www.hachette.co.uk

Twinkle
Makes a Wish

Katharine Holabird and Sarah Warburton

Hodder Children's Books

It was almost Twinkle's birthday and she wanted to invite everyone to her party.

"Come and join me at the Fairy Glen, under the Sparkle Tree. It's going to be a fairytastic birthday jamboree!"

Twinkle was in such a tizzy – there was so much to do before the big day!
Luckily her best friends, Pippa and Lulu, were there to help.

"First let's make some
sparkly invitations,"
said Twinkle.

The three little fairies had lots of fun sticking, cutting and colouring together.
There were sparkles and glitter **everywhere!**

When the invitations were done, Twinkle sent them
out by Special Dragon Delivery.

"Fly super fast!" Twinkle told
Scruffy, her pet dragon.

"Now for the decorations," said Twinkle.

The three little fairies swooped **up** and **down**

and all around the Fairy Glen, stringing up brightly coloured lights,

balloons and streamers – they even used a little **magic!**

"Wow, the Fairy Glen looks super duper!" said Pippa.

"It's time to make my favourite pinkberry cake!"
said Twinkle, opening her *Fairy Flavours* cookbook.

Pinkberry
Cake.

FLOUR

Twinkle loved to bake, and the three fairies
followed the recipe very carefully.

But when the cake came out of the oven it was weird and lumpy.
"This calls for some extra **fairy magic**," said Twinkle, swooshing her wand.

"Cakery Bakery
twiddle-tee tweet,
Make my cake look pretty
and sweet!"

But with each swoosh,
Twinkle's cake just got
lumpier and lumpier...

"Don't worry, Twinks,"
said Lulu, "we'll cover it up
with icing."

At last everything was ready for the party.

Twinkle yawned and checked the brilliant night sky before going to bed.

"Glittering gumdrops,"
she said, "tomorrow's going
to be a very special day!"

But in the middle of the night,
while all the forest creatures were asleep,
there was a huge storm in Sparkle Tree Forest.

The wind blew Twinkle's party
decorations helter-skelter, and rain poured down
and soaked Twinkle's birthday cake!

"Slimy salamanders!" sobbed Twinkle,
arriving at the Fairy Glen the next morning.
"My party's a ginormous mess!"

The forest creatures heard Twinkle crying,
and they all came out to help.

Happy Birthday Twinkle

They found the lost party decorations,
but there was no way they could fix
Twinkle's birthday cake in time.

"Don't worry, we'll pretend there's a cake," said Pippa cheerily.

"And we can still have the party," said Lulu, giving her friend a big hug.

Just then Fairy Godmother arrived with a flourish.

"It's your birthday, Twinkle, so I'm granting you a special wish," she said kindly.

Twinkle looked at her friends and all the creatures who had helped her, then she closed her eyes.

"I wish all the fairies and creatures and elves will have lots of fun and enjoy themselves!"

When Twinkle opened her eyes the party lights were shining, the decorations were sparkling, and the table was perfectly set.

Best of all, there was a beautiful **pinkberry birthday cake!**

"Happy birthday, Twinkle," smiled Fairy Godmother.

Twinkle had a fairytastic birthday
after all, playing and dancing in the
moonlight with her forest friends.
Her heart was glowing with happiness,
and her wings were pink as pompoms.

"My special wish came truly true –
we've all had a wonderful time.
Birthdays are the best of fun when
you have great friends like mine!"

twinkly lights

balloons

party hats

birthday cake

birthday bunting

lanterns

fairy friends

surprise present

Enjoy more sparkling Twinkle stories...

By the author of Angelina Ballerina

Twinkle
Makes a Wish
Katharine Holabird and Sarah Warburton

By the author of Angelina Ballerina

Twinkle
Thinks Pink!
Katharine Holabird and Sarah Warburton

By the author of Angelina Ballerina

Twinkle
Katharine Holabird and Sarah Warburton

By the author of Angelina Ballerina

Twinkle
Tames a Dragon
Katharine Holabird and Sarah Warburton